JUNIOR LEAGUE
ZOO LEARNING FUND

About the Junior League of Kansas City, Missouri, Zoo Learning Fund —

In celebration of its 75th anniversary in 1989, the Junior League of Kansas City, Missouri, created the Zoo Learning Fund. The purpose of the fund is to advance our knowledge of the animal kingdom and the role we play in protecting it.

The Zoo Learning Fund will provide a continuing source of financing for the creation, design and implementation of educational programs and informative materials for use at the New Kansas City Zoo, in school classrooms and in homes.

THE MIXED-UP ZOO OF PROFESSOR YAHOO

Written and illustrated by Nate Evans

Published by the Junior League of Kansas City, Missouri, Inc.,
to benefit the Kansas City Zoo Learning Fund

The Junior League of Kansas City, Missouri, Inc., is an organization of women committed to promoting volunteerism and to improving the community through the effective action and leadership of trained volunteers. Its purpose is exclusively educational and charitable.

The Junior League of Kansas City, Missouri, Inc., reaches out to women of all races, religions, and national origins who demonstrate an interest in — and commitment to — volunteerism.

First edition
ISBN 0-9607076-3-8
Library of Congress Catalog Card
No. 92-071679

Special thanks to the zoo children's book committees, Kate Gibson and Ann Sundeen co-chairmen.

Designed by
Debbie Robinson
WRK, Inc.,
Kansas City, Missouri

Typesetting by
Cicero Graphic Resources, Inc.
Kansas City, Kansas

Dedication

To Kerry the Panda
    and Rich the Giraffe;
to Debbie the Gecko,
    you all make me laugh.
You all are so funny;
    you all are my friends.
This story's for you
    from beginning to ends.

"Hear this," said the Queen, glaring down from her throne,
"It's my birthday and I want a zoo of my own!
It's got to be big! It's got to be grand!
It must be the best zoo in all of the land!

"It's all up to you now, Professor Yahoo,
to make sure my queenly desire comes true!
You'd better go do it and just as I've said!
If not, I'm afraid, sir, it's off with your head!"

"**F**ear not, my dear Queen!" said Professor Yahoo.
"It will be as you wish. I know just what to do.
I'll scour the land for the finest of mammals,
I'll bring you a fox or some hairy, humped camels.

"I'll get you some creatures of which you've not heard,
like a horned wildebeest or a blue booby bird."

I'll fill an aquarium with splashing
    sea things,
    like penguins and seals
    and a huge whale that sings!

I'll build you a wonderful zoo,
    and what's more,
I'll have it all done by a quarter-to-four!"

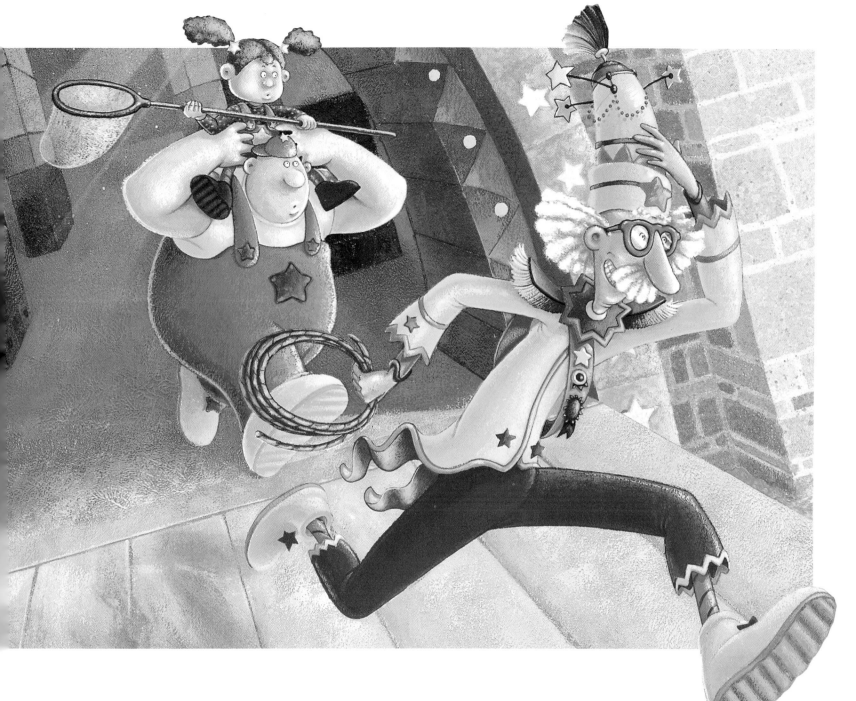

He gathered his helpers, named Bongo and Lu,
and off they all scrambled to build the Queen's zoo.

They ran through the gate and then over the moat,
and that's when old Yahoo...

...tripped over a goat!

He tripped! Wow! He slipped! He fell flat on his face!
And his glasses went flying from their usual place.
They flew off his nose, and they smashed to the ground.
The shattering glass made a terrible sound!

"Yikes!" cried Bongo. And Lu said, "Oh, drat!
Without wearing glasses he's blind as a bat!"

The Professor jumped up. "I can't see now, it's true,
but I'm still the same genius—Professor Yahoo!
I'll still build a zoo that is second to none;
I don't need my glasses to get this job done!"

So looking for wild things, they charged down the road;
   they were searching for bears or a big jungle toad.
They were looking for tigers or monkeys or shrews.
   They were looking for rhinos or red kangaroos.

"Look!" cried Professor Yahoo, pointing right.
   "There's a fierce, yellow lion that's ready to bite!"

"Where is it?" cried Bongo. "Where is it?" cried Lu.
   "We don't see a large, scary lion in view!"

"It's right there, you big goofs! Use a little brain power!"
     "But Professor," cried Lu, "that's a big, yellow...

...flower!"

"It's a lion, I tell you, all set for a fight!
Just box it up quickly, before it can bite!"

So that's what they did, then continued their search.
They were looking for sloths or macaws on a perch.

"**G**adzooks!" the professor exclaimed with a shout.
"That's an elephant there! You can tell by its snout!"

"Professor," cried Lu, "that's no elephant's nose!
It's a...

...fat fire chief with a fireman's hose!"

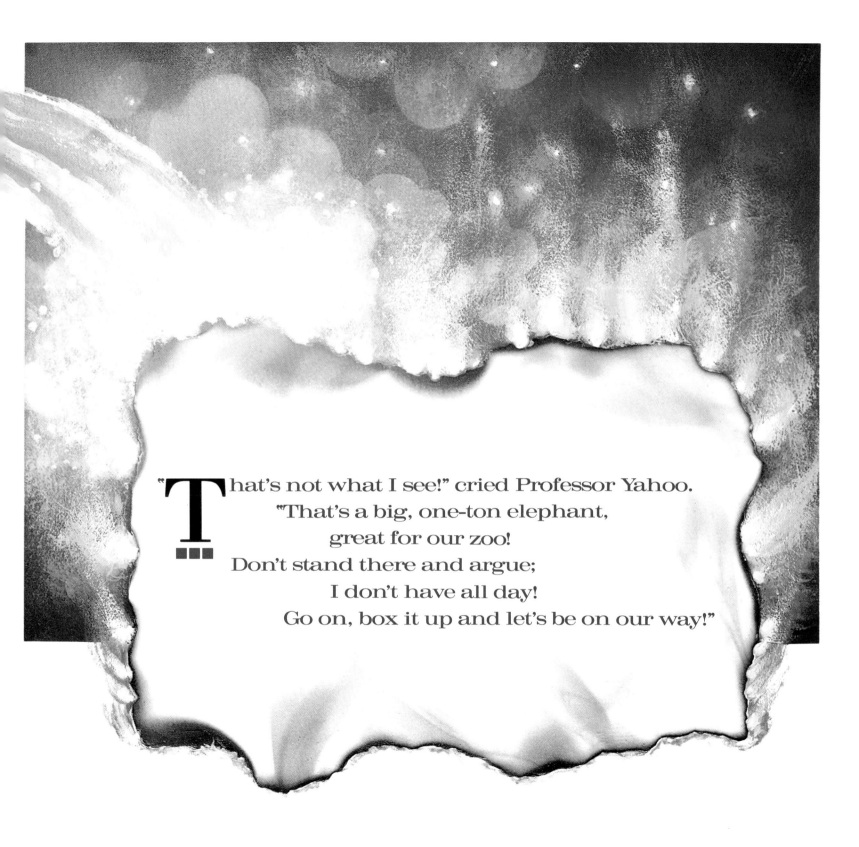

"That's not what I see!" cried Professor Yahoo.
"That's a big, one-ton elephant,
great for our zoo!
Don't stand there and argue;
I don't have all day!
Go on, box it up and let's be on our way!"

S o that's how it went for poor Bongo and Lu.
Just being assistants, well, what could they do?

It was one crazy mix-up right after another—
they captured a pickle and somebody's mother!

They captured a mailbox, a swing set, some spoons.
They snared a T.V. that was showing cartoons.

And he didn't stop there, that silly Yahoo—
he made them catch kites!
What a weird thing to do!

At last Yahoo said, "That's enough. Time to quit."
Lu whispered to Bongo, "I'm having a fit!

"We've got all this stuff, but it's goofy! It's tacky!
The Queen's going to think we've gone totally wacky!"

But what could they do except lug it all back;
they used seven wagons and one grocery sack.

■■■ They took it all back and then set up the zoo.

"I did a great job!" cried Professor Yahoo.

A nd then—oh, good grief!—it was quarter-to-four,
and the Queen stepped majestically out the back door.

"We're goners!" croaked Bongo, his face turning blue.
With a whimper he tried to hide behind Lu.

"I want my zoo now!" cried the Queen, glaring down.
She would have said more, but...

...she tripped on her clown!

She flopped on her face, right into the dirt,
and everyone gasped, "Is the royal Queen hurt?"

"I'm fine!" huffed the Queen, "not one hair out of place!
So you better not laugh; wipe that grin off your face!

"Now show me my zoo! That's my queenly command!
And just as I said, it had better be grand!"

Poor Bongo and Lu were too frightened to look.
They knew they were done for!
Yikes, how their knees shook!

Then Professor Yahoo showed the Queen her strange zoo,
but all that she said was: "Aah!" "Wowee!" and "Ooo!"

"I don't understand," Bongo whispered to Lu.
"The Queen seems to like this mixed-up, crazy zoo!"

L u let loose a giggle, then she started to cheer,
　　　and here's what she said into Bongo's left ear:

■■■　"You saw the Queen slip and go tumbling down.
　　　Her glasses were lost when she fell on her crown!

　　　She's blind as a mole, but is too proud to say!
　　　And that's why she thinks this weird zoo is okay!"

T hen the Queen squinted and said, "Oh, my word!"
She gawked and she cried, "Why, it's some kind of bird!

"Guards, quick, catch this thing! Who let it get loose?
It's some kind of stork or a skinny, old goose!"

■■■

"It's me!" cried Professor Yahoo with a squawk,
      and the Queen cried, "Good heavens! That goose, it can talk!

"**D**on't let it escape! That goose is a star!
It'll make my zoo famous, the best zoo by far!"

Goose

So Professor Yahoo now resides in the zoo,
   where he's fed and he's cared for by Bongo and Lu.

And if you see the Queen, you had better beware;
   she may think you're a chimp or a soft, fuzzy bear.

She may think you're a wombat! Believe it, it's true,
   and you could end up...in the zoo with Yahoo.

About the Author —

Nate Evans, who also wears glasses, was born in Colorado. He grew up in California, spent a few summers in New York City with his father and went to college in Georgia. He then went to Kansas City, Missouri, to work for Hallmark Cards, Inc., where he drew funny animals and met a lot of nice people.

He now lives in Colorado again, where he still is drawing funny animals. He has a very mean cat named Max (because he is a "wild thing") and a best friend named Brenda (who is a human being).

Wherever Nate lives he likes going to the zoo and seeing all the animals (especially the seals and the monkeys . . . and the elephant . . . and also the polar bears . . . and the giraffes).

His heroes are: Daniel Pinkwater, James Marshall, and, of course, the late Dr. Seuss. He sends a special elephant-sized "Thank You" to Mr. Kurt Liesner for some last-minute artistic assistance.

This is Nate's first book and he hopes kids will like it very much.

Additional copies of *The Mixed-Up Zoo of Professor Yahoo* may be ordered by writing to: The Yahoo! Office, 9215 Ward Parkway, Kansas City, MO 64114, or by calling (816) 444-1070.